THE TALE OF THE TWO MOUNTAINS

DO GOOD IF YOU DON'T WANT NIGHTMARES TO TERRIFY YOU AT NIGHT

HARSIMRAN KAUR

ISBN 979-888521890-0

Contents

1

Dwarfs and Hunfs

High on a hill, sat two mountains protected by strong magic of dwarfs (short human like creatures) and hunfs (creatures with some features of animals). Dwarfs lived at their dwarfy mountain and protect their mountain by their dwarfy magic . They used to make good and bad dreams . Dwarfs had a magical long ,bleached and sticky beard . They wore a long coat with two pockets in which they put there hand and pulled out things they want to use for making dreams .The left pocket of their coat always contained those creepy things which they used to make nightmares.

The right pocket of their coat contained the great smelling items they used for making good dreams. They made the dreams by using their magic spells(shaka laka boom boom), a hair from there beard per dream and some magical items. They used a large and a horrified pot to make dreams ,a super tasty potion for good dreams and a super bitter tonic for nightmare. They chanted their spells continuosly and took a hair from their long ,bleached and sticky beard to put it in the large pot and make dreams .

ᐁᐁᐁ

On the other side Hunfs lived at their hunfy mountain and protect their mountain by their hunfy magic. They helped the dwarfs to supply their dreams to the humans in the form of bubble rain.They called the name mr. sky 5 times to inform mr. sky that they have some dwarfy dreams for him to supply them to humans. he had a fluffy and humourless face with bottom down U lips

They had a talking clanging windy machine. She was expert in making excuses and tolerate the tantrums of mr. sky , the dreamy bubbles were dumped in that machine and the machine will spue the bubbles up to mr. sky by singing a song for him as he was a drama king who always wanted everyone's constant attention.

The two fairies of the dwarfy mountain brought the dwarfy dreams in their large bag to the hunfy mountain and the two fairies of the hunfy mountains took the dreams enclosed in magical bubbles to their hunfy mountain. Then the hunfs sent the dreamy bubbles to mr.sky by calling his name 5 times "mr sky mr sky mr sky mr sky mr skyyy " .

After tolerating a lot of tantrums of mr sky. He takes the dreams from the hunfs and lashes down those bubbles in the form of drops to humans.When the drop or the bubble pops, the dream fall out and starts making humans dream . In these bubbles there were ,the good dreams for good people and the bad dreams for bad people.

◁◁◁

2

The Triplets

Both of the dwarfs and the hunfs had an informer . The name of the dwarfy informer was Matilda and the hunfy informer was called Mariam. They travelled to the humans and informed the dwarfs and the hunfs about the good humans and the bad humans . Good dreams were for people who did good deeds and the nightmares were for the bad people.

One day they were roaming around in a park where children were playing. Mariam and Malinda were so tiny that the grass was hardly reaching their waist. They were noticing every child in the park and suddenly saw 3 children quarreling with a girl and saying her to leave the park and play somewhere else and also pushed her.

Matilda said "should we go and help her" but Mariam said "no , we are not allowed to do it" because they weren't allowed to go in front of humans. For a while , They thought about that and decided to notice her next day and said "if she'll be a good child we'll help her out ", and they went back to their own mountains .

When Matilda got there , her one of the dwarfy friend Anna asked her "so what you did today" and Matilda replied "we saw three children fighting with a quiet and sweet girl" Anna said " Oooooo ! so you should do something to help her" "yes we will inform this to our senior dwarfs and tell them to make three little nightmares for them" Anna said "this will be their suitable punishment" and went back to her work. .

The next day both the informers followed that girl the way to her school .They saw her feeding some ants from her own tiffin and picking some wrappers to put them into the dustbin ,by watching this they were confirmed that she was a good girl . They decided to help her by taking revenge from those three children who hurt her. Matilda hurried back to her mountain and told the dwarfs to make 3 little bad dreams for those three.

It took time to make the dreams but when they were ready Matilda took the fairy bag and the dreams with her back.Mariam was waiting all the day for her to come back and finally saw her running towards him . It was night time, they took the nightmares and first went to the bad children's house . Matilda said "I think that they are brothers because I always saw them together and they are almost looking the same" "yes they can be " replied Mariam . Matilda and Mariam entered the house and saw them having their dinner together.Mariam said "you were right , they are triplet brothers ".

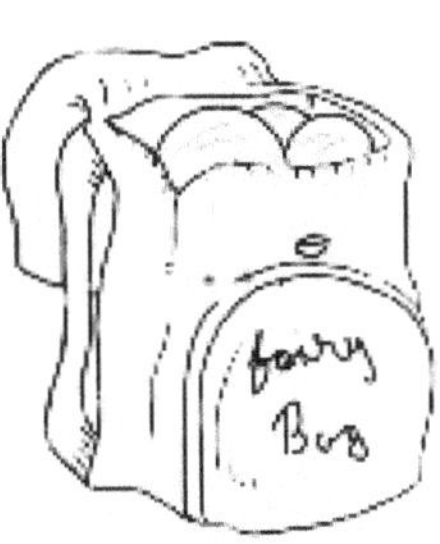

by saying this, mariam rolled towards the stairs, matilda followed him.They crossed the stairs very easily but since they were too small they were not able to open the door of the triplet's bedroom. So they decided to wait for someone to open the door of the bedroom. All the members of the family had just started there dinner and it will take so much time for someone to come upstairs and open the door . Matilda was unable to wait and started searching another way to enter the room.

Then they noticed that there is some space for them under the door from where they can enter the room. They crawled and crawled and finally there mission was completed . They hurridly placed the dreams under the pillow of the triplets and again crawled out of the room and got out of the house.The triplets had a very hard and scary night. but They got the fruit of their deeds .

THE TALE OF THE TWO MOUNTAINS

DO GOOD IF YOU DON'T WANT NIGHTMARES TO TERRIFY YOU AT NIGHT

HARSIMRAN KAUR

ISBN 979-888521890-0

Contents

1

Dwarfs and Hunfs

High on a hill, sat two mountains protected by strong magic of dwarfs (short human like creatures) and hunfs (creatures with some features of animals). Dwarfs lived at their dwarfy mountain and protect their mountain by their dwarfy magic . They used to make good and bad dreams . Dwarfs had a magical long ,bleached and sticky beard . They wore a long coat with two pockets in which they put there hand and pulled out things they want to use for making dreams .The left pocket of their coat always contained those creepy things which they used to make nightmares.

The right pocket of their coat contained the great smelling items they used for making good dreams. They made the dreams by using their magic spells(shaka laka boom boom), a hair from there beard per dream and some magical items. They used a large and a horrified pot to make dreams ,a super tasty potion for good dreams and a super bitter tonic for nightmare. They chanted their spells continuosly and took a hair from their long ,bleached and sticky beard to put it in the large pot and make dreams .

ᐅᐅᐅ

On the other side Hunfs lived at their hunfy mountain and protect their mountain by their hunfy magic. They helped the dwarfs to supply their dreams to the humans in the form of bubble rain.They called the name mr. sky 5 times to inform mr. sky that they have some dwarfy dreams for him to supply them to humans. he had a fluffy and humourless face with bottom down U lips

They had a talking clanging windy machine. She was expert in making excuses and tolerate the tantrums of mr. sky , the dreamy bubbles were dumped in that machine and the machine will spue the bubbles up to mr. sky by singing a song for him as he was a drama king who always wanted everyone's constant attention.

The two fairies of the dwarfy mountain brought the dwarfy dreams in their large bag to the hunfy mountain and the two fairies of the hunfy mountains took the dreams enclosed in magical bubbles to their hunfy mountain. Then the hunfs sent the dreamy bubbles to mr.sky by calling his name 5 times "mr sky mr sky mr sky mr sky mr skyyy " .

After tolerating a lot of tantrums of mr sky. He takes the dreams from the hunfs and lashes down those bubbles in the form of drops to humans. When the drop or the bubble pops, the dream fall out and starts making humans dream . In these bubbles there were ,the good dreams for good people and the bad dreams for bad people.

▷▷▷

2

The Triplets

Both of the dwarfs and the hunfs had an informer . The name of the dwarfy informer was Matilda and the hunfy informer was called Mariam. They travelled to the humans and informed the dwarfs and the hunfs about the good humans and the bad humans . Good dreams were for people who did good deeds and the nightmares were for the bad people.

One day they were roaming around in a park where children were playing. Mariam and Malinda were so tiny that the grass was hardly reaching their waist. They were noticing every child in the park and suddenly saw 3 children quarreling with a girl and saying her to leave the park and play somewhere else and also pushed her.

Matilda said "should we go and help her" but Mariam said "no , we are not allowed to do it" because they weren't allowed to go in front of humans. For a while , They thought about that and decided to notice her next day and said "if she'll be a good child we'll help her out ", and they went back to their own mountains .

When Matilda got there , her one of the dwarfy friend Anna asked her "so what you did today" and Matilda replied "we saw three children fighting with a quiet and sweet girl" Anna said " Oooooo ! so you should do something to help her" "yes we will inform this to our senior dwarfs and tell them to make three little nightmares for them" Anna said "this will be their suitable punishment" and went back to her work. .

The next day both the informers followed that girl the way to her school .They saw her feeding some ants from her own tiffin and picking some wrappers to put them into the dustbin ,by watching this they were confirmed that she was a good girl . They decided to help her by taking revenge from those three children who hurt her. Matilda hurried back to her mountain and told the dwarfs to make 3 little bad dreams for those three.

It took time to make the dreams but when they were ready Matilda took the fairy bag and the dreams with her back.Mariam was waiting all the day for her to come back and finally saw her running towards him . It was night time, they took the nightmares and first went to the bad children's house . Matilda said "I think that they are brothers because I always saw them together and they are almost looking the same" "yes they can be " replied Mariam . Matilda and Mariam entered the house and saw them having their dinner together.Mariam said "you were right , they are triplet brothers ".

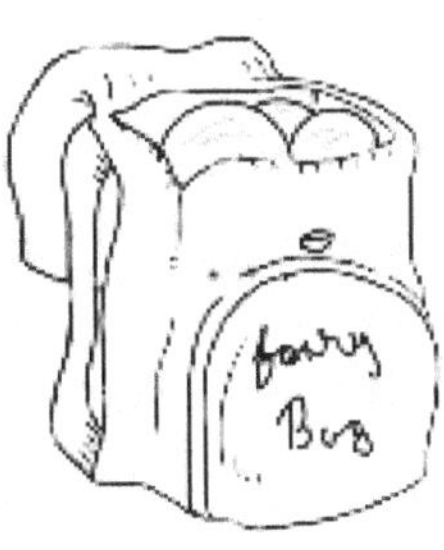

by saying this, mariam rolled towards the stairs, matilda followed him.They crossed the stairs very easily but since they were too small they were not able to open the door of the triplet's bedroom. So they decided to wait for someone to open the door of the bedroom. All the members of the family had just started there dinner and it will take so much time for someone to come upstairs and open the door . Matilda was unable to wait and started searching another way to enter the room.

Then they noticed that there is some space for them under the door from where they can enter the room. They crawled and crawled and finally there mission was completed . They hurridly placed the dreams under the pillow of the triplets and again crawled out of the room and got out of the house.The triplets had a very hard and scary night. but They got the fruit of their deeds .